The Volcano Challenge

The BEAR GRYLLS ADVENTURES series

The Blizzard Challenge
The Desert Challenge
The Jungle Challenge
The Sea Challenge
The River Challenge
The Earthquake Challenge
The Volcano Challenge
The Safari Challenge
The Cave Challenge
The Mountain Challenge

The Volcano Challenge

Bear Grylls

Illustrated by Emma McCann

Bear Grylls

First American Edition 2019
Kane Miller, A Division of EDC Publishing

First published in Great Britain in 2018 by Bear Grylls, an imprint of
Bonnier Zaffre, a Bonnier Publishing Company
Text and illustrations copyright © Bear Grylls Ventures, 2018
Illustrations by Emma McCann

For information contact:
Kane Miller, A Division of EDC Publishing
PO Box 470663
Tulsa, OK 74147-0663
www.kanemiller.com
www.edcpub.com
www.usbornebooksandmore.com

Library of Congress Control Number: 2018946376

Printed and bound in the United States of America
2 3 4 5 6 7 8 9 10

ISBN: 978-1-68464-041-6

To the young survivor
reading this book for the first time.
May your eyes always be wide open
to adventure, and your heart full
of courage and determination to
see your dreams through.

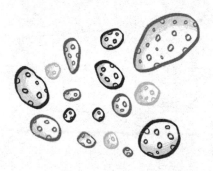

1

MAGMA QUEST

The ground shook. Chunks of fire flew through the air.

Charlie ducked and dodged, getting out of the way of the flying fragments.

Wherever they hit the ground, they blasted everything away, leaving a crater full of molten rock.

"Charlie ..."

Charlie ignored the voice. He had to concentrate. A blazing boulder was coming right for him. He was going too fast to stop. It was too late to swerve. The boulder smashed into the ground right in front of him, leaving a deadly crater of bubbling lava.

One touch would mean instant death.

Charlie only had one choice.

Jump.

One, two, three …

"Charlie!"

Charlie looked up. He was sitting at a picnic table in a forest clearing with his friends Joe, Harry and Olly. They were at camp. There were no flying rocks or craters. But two of his friends were looking worried.

"We just got the five-minute warning," Harry said.

"And we're on cleanup today, Charlie,

remember?" Olly added.

Charlie had been too busy playing Magma Quest on his tablet to actually eat anything. He grabbed his bacon with one hand, and looked again at the screen. His character crunched face-first into the crater.

Game over.

"Ugh!" he groaned. "I never get across that crater!"

Harry pretended to give an enormous yawn. Olly dropped his head to one side

and started to snore loudly. Joe smiled.

"Tell us something new," he said kindly. "You're obsessed!"

Olly pushed back from the table and picked his tray up.

"See you over there, Charlie?" he said.

Charlie swallowed some bread and washed it down with juice as he watched the others walk off. He still had a banana to eat. Maybe he could have one more try while he finished his breakfast?

Bananas! Charlie thought suddenly. Bananas were slippery, weren't they? Maybe that was the trick. If he played in antigravity mode then he could make his character skid a little. That way he'd just glide along …

Charlie licked his fingers clean and restarted the level. He'd just

dodged his first flying
boulder when…

"Charlie? Charlie!"

He looked up.

Everyone on cleanup duty was waiting
for him on the other side of the clearing.
There were more picnic tables covered
with plates and pots and pans. The
leader was smiling. Kind of.

"Oh, sorry … hang on …" Charlie
called. Just a couple more seconds should
do it…

"Charlie, *now!*" the leader called,
sounding annoyed. "Put that away!"

Charlie reluctantly paused the game.
As he walked over to the others he could
almost hear Magma Quest calling him.
All he needed was another try and he'd
smash it this time…

"Right!" The leader clapped his hands together and gave them all a big smile. "Let's get started."

Charlie could feel himself getting annoyed. If he didn't have to bother with this silly cleanup he could finish the level.

"Gather everything up," said the leader. "Uneaten food into compost bags, cutlery into this basket here. Plates

can be heavy, so don't carry more than five at a time, please. You can work in pairs…"

Charlie could feel his chance to play Magma Quest slipping away and his bad mood get worse.

"Charlie and Fatima, you two can work together …"

Great, thought Charlie. His shoulders slumped. This really was game over.

Fatima and Charlie took opposite sides of the table. Charlie picked up a couple of plates, and felt his thumb squelch into a blob of butter and jam. *Yuck!* He looked up at Fatima. She was busy working. It would only take thirty seconds. He could get over the crater, get the level out of the way, then get on with cleanup.

Charlie pulled the tablet out. His character wobbled on the edge of the crater, then tumbled into the fire at the bottom before Charlie could react. Another life down!

His character reappeared on the other side of the field. He aimed at the crater again, started to run …

"Charlie!" Fatima was staring at him from beside a neatly stacked pile of plates, clearly annoyed.

He looked back at the screen and groaned. He'd lost another life. And now Fatima was nagging him as well.

"Sorry, *Mom*," Charlie muttered sarcastically. He paused the game *again*. He chucked cutlery into the bowl and piled the plates up. Uneaten food squished out between them.

"You're meant to scrape the food off first," said Fatima.

Charlie ran out of patience.

"You do it then," he snapped angrily. He sat down and went back to Magma Quest. He knew he was being bad-tempered, but he couldn't help himself. He just wanted to

finish the level – and she was interrupting him. It was so annoying.

"Charlie!"

It was the leader. He plucked the game out of Charlie's hands.

"Concentrate on your job," he told Charlie firmly. "You can play this later."

"That is so unfair!" Charlie protested, crashing the plates together crossly. He looked up just in time to see Fatima try to pick up a pile of plates that was way too big for her to manage on her own.

The pile slipped through her fingers and smashed onto the ground.

Crash!

Charlie felt bad. Maybe it was partly his fault Fatima had tried to carry all those plates. He'd been horrible to her when she'd tried to get him to help.

He went over to see if he could help her clean up.

"Lucky you were wearing your boots," he said, looking down at the sharp fragments of broken plates. "It could have really hurt, otherwise." He paused. "You okay?"

Fatima was still gazing down at her feet. Eventually she looked up.

"Yes, I'm fine. And uh, thanks, Charlie."

Charlie started clearing and piling everything up correctly. He didn't want to cause another accident. They worked as a team and soon caught up.

The leader was pleased with both of them at the end. He held the tablet out and Charlie almost snatched it out of his hand. There was still a bit of time before capture the flag...

"Hey, Charlie?" Fatima said. "Want to see something cool?"

"Mm?" Charlie didn't look up. He was sprinting through a field of craters and flying fireballs. Just a few more seconds …

It worked! The antigravity slide took him right over the crater.

Fatima put something on the table next to him. Charlie saved the game and looked up. It looked like a weird watch in a thick rubber case, but without a strap.

He turned it over in his fingers. No buttons. No screen. It looked boring. "What does it do?"

Fatima smiled.

"Perhaps you'll find out?" she said. "Just consider it a gift. A compass can come in handy."

"Uh – thanks. Maybe I can use it in capture the flag?"

"Well, you'd better get going in that case," Fatima laughed. "They're starting in a couple of minutes…"

Charlie liked capture the flag a lot. There was no time to take his tablet back to the tent, and he sprinted away from the clearing. There was no way he was going to miss the start.

2

CAPTURE THE FLAG

Everyone was standing around the mound in the middle of the clearing with a flag planted in it. A couple of leaders were drawing names out of a hat while everyone watched and crossed their fingers.

"Jack," the leader called.

Jack grinned and went to stand over to one side.

"Susie ... Adam ..."

Meanwhile another leader was handing out Velcro armbands to everyone else.

"Okay," the leader called, "the rules are simple. The clue is in the name! Capture the flag – without being caught. These ten here are the guardians. They defend the flag. If they pull your armband off then you become a guardian yourself."

"Smart," Charlie said to Harry and Joe.

"So every time someone gets caught, the number of guardians goes up and it gets harder for everyone else."

The best games always got harder as they went on. It was never any fun if things were too easy.

Charlie looked over at the stream that ran on one side of the clearing. He whispered to Harry and Joe, "I have a plan."

The boys rolled their eyes. Charlie was always so serious about strategy.

The leader blew his whistle. Everyone with an armband turned and ran for the trees. Charlie put a hand on each of his friends' shoulders. "Follow me."

***

The plan almost worked.

Charlie had led the boys through the woods and then doubled back to the stream. He was good at remembering directions. After all, he'd played enough computer games to know how important it was to remember layouts of levels and rooms. As they'd moved through the trees he'd pictured a map in his head of where they'd been.

They'd moved carefully, keeping their eyes peeled for guardians. They'd heard shouts of triumph and frustration. With every yell they knew that more players were being caught, and more guardians were being created.

They'd followed the stream toward the clearing.

When Charlie had seen the stream it had reminded him of a computer game he had at home, Under Siege. You had to work against the clock to defend your castle from attack, and one of the best ways was to dig a moat to protect yourself. If you were behind a moat, nothing could get you. It had given him an idea.

"So what we do," Charlie had explained, "is two of us go up to the clearing and we let the guardians see us. They'll come running, but they won't want to get wet so they'll run along the stream on the other side until they can get across. Meanwhile, one of us who doesn't mind getting wet gets across the stream and captures the flag!"

He'd volunteered to be one of the decoys – he didn't want to risk dropping his tablet in the stream. Harry was going to go for the flag while Charlie and Joe distracted the guardians and made them run after them on the other side of the stream.

"Intruders!"

They had been spotted. Jack and Fatima burst through the trees ahead and charged forward. But instead of running alongside the stream, Jack and Fatima both splashed straight into the water, kicking it up as they charged, with huge grins on their faces.

"Split!" Joe shouted, and they all ran off in separate directions.

Charlie hurdled over logs and tree roots, wondering why his plan hadn't worked. The strategy was perfect in Under Siege. Why had it failed in capture the flag?

Okay, people were always telling him that computer games weren't like real life, but he had been so sure …

Charging through the woods was like racing through the levels on Magma Quest, only in real life there was more mud and a lot more effort required. He wished he could use antigravity mode now. He felt the tablet slipping around in his pocket, and he grabbed it as he jumped another ditch.

He was back at the campfire clearing, where last night's bonfire was still smoldering in the middle. A small trickle of gray smoke drifted up from the pile of ash. Now that he was on his own, Charlie needed to come up with a new plan to get him back to the flag. He crouched down behind a pile of logs, and pictured the map in his head.

The flag clearing was on the north side of the woods. But which way was north? It would so be handy to have a digital map right now, like the tiny one in the corner of the screen on Magma Quest. He could just pinch it and zoom in on exactly where he was. Or even just a compass icon on screen like in …

A compass! Fatima had given him one. Charlie dug into his pocket and pulled it out. Maybe it really was going to be useful after all.

He looked at the dial. It was weird. This one had five points on it, not the usual four. And the needle was just spinning around and around. Well, that was useless. No wonder Fatima hadn't wanted it.

Charlie looked up and saw wood smoke from the fire coming straight at him. But not just a trickle, a huge great cloud. In a moment, the smoke was black and dense, covering him completely. His eyes stung and his lungs burned. It didn't smell like wood either. It stank like rotten eggs. Burnt rotten eggs. It was the most disgusting thing Charlie had ever smelled. His eyes streamed with tears, and he bent double, gagging and coughing.

Then the smoke began to clear and Charlie waved a hand in front of his face.

Through his damp, sore eyes he looked around with amazement.

He wasn't at camp.

Charlie was standing on a slope of dark-gray rock. The rock sloped gently in front of him, then fell sharply away. Charlie edged forward just enough to see that he was hundreds of feet up in the air. Maybe half a mile or more. Far, far below him was a flat, gray desert, the color of ash. He searched the horizon in front of him, but all he could see was gray rock stretching as far as the eye could see. Here and there puffs of smoke jetted up out of the ground. There were no trees. No plants. Not one scrap of life was visible.

It looked like the surface of the Moon.

Out of the corner of his eye, Charlie saw a flash of color. He jerked his head around.

A stream of red-hot lava was flowing down the slope about two hundred feet behind him. He could feel its warmth on his skin.

Charlie looked up.

"Argh!"

What he had seen had terrified him. He recoiled and instantly crouched down. He was sure a million tons of rock was about to fall down on him, just like in Magma Quest.

Charlie was very near the summit of a giant volcano. The top of the mountain was jagged, like a broken tooth, and the lava stream was pouring out through one of the gaps. Thick, black smoke rose up behind it in a column. It must have been a mile high and a billion times thicker than the wood smoke at camp. It looked so solid. It looked *impossible.* How could all those rocks be falling upward? Charlie was paralyzed with fear.

Then a man's voice spoke, right behind him.

"We need to get off this mountain. It could explode again any minute."

3

EXACTLY ONE LIFE EACH

Charlie whipped his head around and stared.

The man was tall and tanned, dressed in tough-looking clothes and wearing a pair of clear wraparound goggles. He was tilting his head back and looking up at the smoke.

"Even if the volcano doesn't explode, that cloud is something we definitely want to get away from."

Charlie stared up at it. It looked even more scary now.

"It's a mix of ash and rubble, and all that's holding it up is hot air. The moment it cools it'll come crashing down."

Definitely more scary.

"Did you ever hear of Pompeii?" said the man, looking at Charlie. "A huge great cloud of ash from the Vesuvius volcano buried the city of Pompeii in seconds, even though it was ten miles away."

The man grinned at Charlie.

"Mind you, Pompeii was also downwind of Vesuvius. We're upwind, so it should

30

fall away from us."

"What ... how ...?" Charlie stammered. "Where are we?"

He was *meant* to be in a clearing in the woods at camp. He was *meant* to be playing capture the flag. This must be a really bad dream.

The man seemed pretty real, though. "We're on the side of a massive volcano," he said calmly. "And like I said, we need to get off it." He held out his hand. "I'm Bear, and I'm going to help guide you out of here."

"I'm Charlie. But ..." Charlie stood up cautiously and turned around in a slow circle. He saw the ash and the mountain and the lava. He *must* be dreaming. "This volcano was in my game," he said. He showed Bear the tablet. "I've just finished this level on Magma Quest. I won five more lives, and super strength, and antigravity."

"Well, sport, now you're on a volcano for real," Bear said kindly. "We're going to have to get out of here with just our usual strength and regular gravity. And exactly one life each."

His words might have sounded grim, but his face was reassuring.

"So, are you ready for some real adventure?" Bear asked.

"Um," Charlie murmured. His voice sounded far away. "Okay."

"That's the spirit," said Bear. "You know, Charlie, survival starts with telling yourself that you can do it." Bear took a step back and looked him up and down. "And after that, the most important thing is having the right gear. Your glasses are good – they'll protect your eyes from grit. But you'll need something tougher than jeans and a T-shirt."

Bear shrugged his backpack onto the ground and shoved his hands into it. A few moments later he had produced clothes just like the ones he was wearing, only a few sizes smaller. There was a shirt, some pants in a tough material, and a thick, waterproof jacket. There was a pair of gloves as well, and Charlie noticed for the first time that Bear was wearing a pair too.

"It's not cold enough for those, is it?" said Charlie.

"Cold lava can be razor sharp," said Bear. "So the best rule is no bare skin, apart from your face. And we might feel warm now, but later on the wind will cut right through us without a good coat. Oh, and you'll need these too."

He set down a pair of Charlie-sized leather boots.

"I've got my sneakers on," Charlie said.

"They're very nice, but they're no good for up here, I'm afraid." Bear scuffed one of his own boots across the ground and made a small ditch in the loose covering of ash. "You see how crumbly and unstable the ground is? Without proper ankle support you might twist your foot and end up with a sprain. Even if you don't, your sneakers will fill up with loose ash. It looks soft, but it's not like ash from a wood fire. It's more like broken glass. It'll grind into your skin with every step. Trust me, you don't want that."

Charlie reached out for the boots.

When he'd changed, Charlie passed Bear his sneakers and his old clothes to put in the backpack. But he was still holding on to his tablet. "Shall I look after that too?" Bear asked. "You'll never find it again if you drop it up here."

Charlie knew the tablet would be safer in Bear's backpack, but he hated handing it over.

"Sure," he said. The word caught in his dry throat and he coughed. He hadn't realized how thirsty he was.

"It's dry up here, huh?" Bear said. "The air just sucks the moisture out of you. We'll need to keep ourselves hydrated."

Bear handed him a water bottle and they each took a swig. Then Bear hoisted his backpack onto his back and pointed down the slope.

"See how there's a ridge of rock zigzagging downhill?" he asked. "We'll stick to that. It's slightly higher than the rest of the ground, so there won't be as much ash on it and it should be pretty solid. When you walk, do it like this."

Bear bent his knees so that he was crouching slightly.

"It lowers your center of gravity, so there's less far to drop with each footstep. Give it a try."

Charlie copied him.

"It feels a bit weird," he said.

Bear laughed. "You're right. But your body will soon get used to it. And you're doing great, by the way."

Charlie smiled. The panicky feeling was easing a little now that he was actually doing something.

Bear put a hand on his shoulder. "Right, Charlie. Off we go."

They headed down the slope in single

file, Bear in front. Charlie had the feeling there was a massive bomb behind him. On a countdown. Ticking down to zero.

He took a quick look over his shoulder at the volcano.

They would have to do a *lot* of walking to be a safe distance away.

As he was turning back around, Charlie felt his foot slip. For a moment he thought he was going to fall, but he managed to steady himself.

"You okay there, buddy?" said Bear.

"Fine." Bear had been right about the ground. The loose ash was crumbly and slippery. Charlie vowed to be more careful from now on.

They carried on for a few minutes more until they reached the ridge. It sloped down pretty steeply, and

Bear was walking with his knees bent in front. It looked really odd. Charlie decided to straighten up. He was sure he'd go quicker if he did it his way.

Very soon Charlie's legs felt like they had hot lava running through them. Then the ache spread up into his back. Every step he took downhill sent an extra judder into his spine.

Reluctantly, he tried walking Bear's way again. The ache moved down from his back and into his

legs, but that was okay. It was just the feeling of his muscles working. At least his steps didn't shudder anymore. Bear turned around and gave him a smile.

Soon they came to a bit where the slope got shallower if they turned left. Charlie followed it with his eyes.

But Bear kept going down the steep part.

"Um – wouldn't it be easier that way?" Charlie asked.

"The path might be easier to walk, but that way would take us downwind," Bear said. "As long as we stay upwind, any poisonous gases from the crater will blow away from us."

"Poisonous gases?" Charlie asked, alarmed. There hadn't been any of those in Magma Quest.

"Carbon monoxide, usually," Bear said. "You can't see it or taste it, but one good whiff can suffocate you in seconds. Even if it just disorientates you or makes you sleepy, that could be fatal at the wrong moment. So if you find yourself feeling really sleepy, you'll let me know, won't you?"

Charlie nodded and swallowed nervously.

He followed slowly after Bear, careful to put his feet in exactly the same places.

The slope was steep and it took all his concentration. At least it kept his mind from freaking out about invisible clouds of poisonous gas drifting down on them.

"But you know," said Bear after a

41

while, "not all gases come from the top. Some might suddenly spurt out of a hole in the side of the mountain ..."

Poisonous gases, Charlie thought. A column of ash that could crush them. Streams of lava that could roast you alive ...

This was *not* what Magma Quest was like.

He wondered what other dangers were waiting for them.

4

GLACIAL PROGRESS

Charlie and Bear spent the next hour trudging down the mountain. The volcano rumbled and grumbled behind them, a constant and clear reminder of the need to stay alert.

Before long, Charlie saw the ice. At first he assumed it was a narrow band of snow. Then he remembered Magma Quest and knew exactly what it was.

"That's a glacier, right?" he asked.

There was a glacier level in the game, before the lava level. You had to get over a stretch of slippery, slidey ice without skidding over the edge.

"That's right," Bear said. "Think of it as a million-ton river moving very slowly downhill."

"Cool," said Charlie. It looked a whole lot easier than where they'd come from. He imagined they'd soon be sliding over the ice, quickly getting to safety.

As soon as they reached the edge of the glacier, Charlie gasped. It wasn't sparkly white, like in the game. It looked gray, mixed up with ash and dirt. And it didn't look easy either. At the edge of the glacier, it was like they were standing on the edge of the world.

The glacier stretched out in front of

them for about three hundred feet. But it was down to the left that Charlie was staring. The glacier quickly sloped down in a steep drop. The bottom was so far down he could only just see it.

Charlie had seen some awesome stuff on screen, but it couldn't match this view. If he peered over, he could see the slope of the volcano at the bottom, carrying on downward. He took in a couple of lungfuls of the cold air.

"Are we going to climb down?" he asked. He could tell it wouldn't be easy, but surely there would be masses of ridges and handholds in the ice cliff. He reckoned they could do it.

Bear wasn't so sure. "This isn't good," he said grimly as he studied the cliff below.

"Yeah, but isn't it better than back up there?" Charlie asked. Ice was way easier to cross than lava, wasn't it?

"It's too dangerous, Charlie," Bear said as he looked around. "We don't have the right equipment to deal with ice."

"Isn't there a way?" Charlie thought about how there was always a way to complete a level in a game. You just needed to keep trying until you cracked it.

"I'm afraid not," Bear smiled. "Safety first, Charlie. Always. There's no way we can climb over this. Not without risking our necks. And if we fell, even if we survived the fall, the chances are that one of us would have a broken arm or leg. And that would make it even harder for us to get out."

Charlie thought about his game. If you lost a life, you just started again. But as Bear had said, they only had one life each here on this mountain.

"Oh." Charlie tried not to sound disappointed. "Well, at least we tried."

"Absolutely," Bear agreed. "We tried the safest option first. Unfortunately we now have to try a less-safe option."

"But we're still getting off the volcano, right?" Charlie asked. He glanced back the way they had come. The column of black smoke was still rising up from the volcano. Charlie even wondered whether it was looking a bit bigger and darker.

"We are," Bear agreed. "We'll try another way down. See this?" He pointed at a trickle of water at the edge of the ice. "The glacier is melting, and all that warm water runs off somewhere. How about we see if we can find where it goes?"

They walked down the slope, following the water along the edge of the glacier.

The longer they walked, the more Charlie realized that the whole edge of the glacier was turning into water. The ice at the edge was so thin you could see right through to the rocks below. A small stream was flowing downhill next to it, like rainwater running down a gutter.

That's something else Magma Quest got wrong, Charlie thought. In the glacier level, the ice just stayed there. It didn't melt. When he got back to camp, or anywhere near a Wi-Fi signal, he would be leaving a seriously negative review of the game. The game creators obviously didn't know anything about *real* volcanoes.

Eventually the trickle at the side of the glacier got stronger and turned into a small stream.

That's when Bear stopped and pointed. The stream disappeared down a hole in the ice, about three feet wide.

"Well, that settles it, Charlie," he said, a smile spreading across his face. "We can't go over it, so we're just going to have to go under it."

5

A MILLION TONS OF ICE

Charlie stared at the opening where the stream had tunneled into the ice. It was like the entrance to a large rabbit hole, only this one had a stream flowing over the rocks at the bottom and the walls shone with an eerie blue ice.

We're going under? Charlie thought. What had Bear called the glacier? "A million-ton river." And they were going to go *under* it?

He thought for a moment. Bear had said there wasn't any other way. Charlie knew he could trust him.

"Okay then, champ," said Bear, looking him in the eyes. "We'll be crawling through meltwater, so it's going to be really cold in there. There's no way we can avoid getting our hands and knees wet, but we've got to try not to get any wetter than that. And if the tunnel starts getting too narrow, we'll just backtrack."

"Backtrack?"

"Yeah, but I hope it won't come to that. Remember, all this water's going somewhere. Wherever the water's going, we can go there too. Ready?"

Charlie swallowed hard and nodded.

"Sure," he said. He could do this. Couldn't he?

Bear crouched down and went in first. For a moment Charlie wondered whether the tunnel might not be so cold. After all, they were on the side of a volcano, weren't they?

It only took a couple of seconds for Charlie's question to be answered. As soon as the water soaked into Charlie's gloves and through the knees of his pants, he knew that Bear hadn't been kidding. At first his fingers just went numb. Then they started to throb. They had never ached this much before, even when he'd been at home, jamming at keys for hours as he played games into the night. He'd even moaned about it with his friends after a long session – but now he felt silly that he'd ever complained. That discomfort was nothing compared to cold like this.

Thinking about home made him feel funny inside. He wished he could be back there right now.

Charlie knew that he needed to think positive, so he told himself that when he got back, he'd be the only one who could say, "Oh, yeah, once I was up on this volcano, and we got away by crawling through an ice tunnel in the middle of a glacier."

If he was at home, he'd never have had an experience like this. Maybe a bit of discomfort was worth it.

The tunnel sloped gently down, and as they crawled along, Charlie noticed that the sides weren't completely smooth. They were knobbly, and they made Charlie imagine that the glacier was a huge animal and they were crawling along its insides.

A loud, low noise brought him out of his daydream. It was a groan, but he was sure it wasn't coming from him or Bear.

Charlie stopped and listened.

The sound returned, but this time it lasted longer. *Creak – creak – creak.*

"What's that?" he asked. His voice sounded all wobbly.

The tunnel was too narrow for Bear to turn around, but he paused and spoke gently. "It's just the glacier moving. Don't worry, I know it sounds scary, but we're okay."

"Really?"

"Really. It probably moves about three feet a day. That's pretty slow, right?"

Right, thought Charlie. It's nothing to worry about. Just the sound of a million tons of ice moving around over my head.

The deeper they went into the tunnel, the darker it became. There was still the same blue color to the ice, but it was fainter now. That made it even more eerie.

"Um, Bear," he said after a while. "How far do we have to go?"

Bear still couldn't look around to talk, and he was just a dark shape ahead of Charlie. But he stopped crawling and spoke in a calm, gentle tone that Charlie found reassuring. "Well, we know the glacier's about three hundred feet across, up top. But that's straight across, and we're going down, so it will be longer than that. And it twists and turns. So, short answer, can't say. How are you doing, champ?"

"I'm okay," Charlie said. "I think."

He could have said his hands and knees were freezing cold and wet, but what could Bear do about that? He was numb and sore, but he could keep going. He knew that much. That was all that really mattered.

They started moving again, but almost straightaway Bear stopped so suddenly that Charlie nearly crawled into him.

"What is it?" Charlie asked.

"It's decision time, Charlie. The tunnel splits in front. What shall we choose, left or right?"

Charlie thought about this. If this was a game, he'd need to think logically and apply the rules to help him choose. So what rules did they have to follow out here in real life?

"Well, I suppose the water must know which way to go," Charlie said. "It'll still flow downhill – it has to because of gravity."

"Good thinking, sport!" Bear sounded impressed. "And if it was flowing down a blocked tunnel it would just fill up. So, we should follow the stream." Charlie could hear Bear was smiling, without having to see it. "Left it is, then!"

They crawled on and Charlie felt better. It was funny how the cold and the pain were more bearable when he was feeling confident.

The end of the tunnel came suddenly. One moment everything was the usual dim-blue color, and then they came around a corner and the light turned bright white. Daylight was streaming in from ahead. The round tunnel grew wider, but the ceiling closed in and got lower, so low that they had to get right down onto their fronts. They elbowed their way along for the last few feet. Charlie's face was just inches away from the damp grit and gravel.

And then they were through. The ceiling of ice vanished, and Bear was helping Charlie to his feet in the open once more.

"Wow!" said Charlie as he turned around. They were facing a giant cliff of ice. It was so tall that Charlie had to crane his head back to look up to the top. He could still see the column of smoke from the volcano, but the glacier was so big that he couldn't see the top of the mountain itself.

"We came down that?" he exclaimed. "Go, us!"

"Absolutely!" said Bear, grinning. "Definitely easier crawling through it than climbing down it. You did great, Charlie. Really good work. We'll take a break here, then push on.

"Besides," he said, looking down at his and Charlie's soaked legs and hands, "we could both use some drying out."

6

SEE, HEAR, SMELL, TOUCH, TASTE

The water that Bear handed Charlie tasted better than any drink he'd ever had. He'd had no idea he was so thirsty.

"We'll get down onto the lava plain and then keep going for a couple of hours before we stop again," Bear said. "How do you feel about putting some distance between us and the volcano?"

Charlie wiped his mouth and gave

a big thumbs-up. The giant column of smoke looked a little bit thinner, but it still reached right up to the top of the sky. Charlie liked the idea of getting out of range.

They set off down the slope toward the level ground that spread out below. It was a massive stretch of cold lava, completely covered with curving, swirling lines. To Charlie it looked like a close-up of giant fingerprints. But it reminded him of something else as well …

"It's like the Moon," Charlie said.

"You're right, sport. It's exactly like the Moon," Bear agreed. "In fact, NASA uses lava plains like these to test the equipment they're sending to the Moon or to Mars. But right now we need to find our direction. The coast is due south of here and if we head there we should find more people. And even if we don't find anyone straightaway, we'll have plenty more options for staying alive by the sea."

"Hang on." Charlie had remembered the gift Fatima had given him and was now rummaging in Bear's backpack. "Look!" he said as he pulled out the compass. "This'll help, right?"

"Perfect!" Bear smiled. "You can be in charge of navigation."

The last time Charlie had used the compass the needle had been spinning around so fast it was impossible to read. It was calmer now, and had just four directions on the face. Charlie watched the needle carefully and turned until they were facing due south. "It's that way," he said, pointing across the smooth, flat ground.

"You've got it, sport!" said Bear. "How about I go in front at first? Only walk where I walk."

"Is there a problem?" Charlie asked nervously.

"There shouldn't be," Bear said. "But remember, all this was molten lava once. It might still be hot under the surface. When the lava cools it forms a solid crust on top, but if the crust gets too thin our feet could go right through."

Charlie winced. "Ouch."

"Big ouch," said Bear, reaching into his backpack. "So we use this."

Bear pulled out a fancy walking stick that expanded like a telescope. Charlie looked confused. What use was a single stick against molten lava?

"We use it to test each step," said Bear, tapping the ground.

Charlie swallowed. The idea of falling into molten lava was scary. "I'll walk where you walk," he said.

They started out slowly. Bear was careful to test the ground in front of him with the stick, only stepping forward onto a new bit of lava once he was sure that it would hold his weight. Charlie was sure he could feel that the ground was hotter in some places. He was tempted to worry about how thin the crust might be getting, but remembered Bear's advice: *survival starts with telling yourself that you can do it.*

He stopped himself from thinking about whether the ground was hollow. Instead he put his mind on following exactly where Bear walked.

As they went on, the cold lava got darker and rougher. The heat that Charlie thought he could feel through his boots was no longer there. Finally, once Bear was sure the lava was thick enough, they could walk side by side.

Charlie kept an eye on the compass to make sure they still headed due south. In Magma Quest you always knew which way you were heading because there was a rotating compass icon on the screen. Out here, it wasn't so simple.

Then it occurred to Charlie that he didn't have to keep checking the compass. Surely he could pick a landmark in the right direction and head for that?

He fixed his eyes on a hill in the distance. It wasn't a big one. In fact, it was more like a bigger-than-usual bump in the lava. But it was in the right direction, so that was where he would make sure they headed.

Charlie's eyes were dry, and he blinked. When he looked again, he had lost his landmark. There were several big bumps, and they all looked the same. Was it *that* one? Or *that* one?

Charlie sighed, and checked the compass.

"Are you okay?" Bear gave him a questioning look.

"I lost my landmark," Charlie explained. "It all looks so similar out here."

"True. But remember, a landmark can be in any direction. You don't have to be heading toward it."

It took Charlie a moment to work out what he meant.

"Oh! Right!"

He looked around, scanning the horizon. There were just a load of bumps and rocks. He kept turning. Everything looked the same. Except the one absolutely massive landmark that they could never lose …

"If we keep the volcano behind us," he said, "we'll always know we're heading away from it."

"You've got it, Charlie. Well done! But we need to keep checking our course constantly. Can I show you a useful trick?"

He picked up ten small pebbles and tipped them into Charlie's cupped hands.

"Say we want to check our course every five hundred paces," Bear said. "Problem is, it's easy to lose count with big numbers, especially if you have to concentrate on where to

put your feet, and you're getting tired."

"Right," Charlie agreed.

"Using the pebbles helps you keep track," Bear went on. "Put them all in one pocket. Every fifty paces, you move one pebble to your other pocket. That way you only have to count to fifty, not five hundred. When you've moved all ten pebbles over, that's five hundred paces, so you can check our direction."

They walked side by side across the cold lava. Charlie navigated, using Bear's pebble trick. Counting up to fifty, ten times, was much easier than counting up to five hundred. And every time he moved a pebble over he took a quick look to check that the volcano was still directly behind them. Then, every five hundred paces, Charlie got a real sense of accomplishment when he checked their direction on the compass. It wasn't a flashy trick, or anything amazing, but breaking down the journey like this seemed to work. He was feeling confident again. They were going to be off this mountain in no time.

The endless gray landscape seemed to go on for miles. But just when Charlie was about to stop and check his compass for the tenth time, he saw a flash of color nearby. It wasn't much, just a speck of green, but as he got closer he saw that it was a tiny plant pushing its way out of the lava, one leaf at a time.

"Nature's full of tough survivors," said Bear. "Even in the harshest landscapes you can see the most beautiful things."

After that, Charlie started to see color everywhere. Bear pointed out the streaks in the rock that were different minerals. There were insects too, and more plants.

Charlie was amazed. There was stuff out here that he could never get on his tablet screen. And on a screen, if you zoomed in far enough, everything went fuzzy. But out here, the closer you zoomed in, the more fascinating details you saw.

Suddenly, Bear stopped. He seemed to be listening for something.

After a moment, Charlie could hear it too. It was like the groan they'd heard beneath the glacier, only this was way louder. It reached inside his ears and went all the way down through the soles of his boots.

It was the deepest rumble he'd ever heard. And it was getting louder.

"Uh-oh," Bear said, turning to look back at the volcano. The smoke column had gotten even smaller.

"Isn't it going down?" Charlie asked.

"Yes, but not in a good way," said Bear. "Less smoke means there's a blockage somewhere. That noise we can hear means that something is about to …"

Just then the top of the volcano exploded, with a *boom* so loud that it shook Charlie's insides.

"… blow!" Bear shouted.

7

EXTRA PRESSURE

Dark streaks shot out from the volcano in all directions. Charlie watched, frozen to the spot, as a steady stream of rock and ash flew three thousand feet up into the air. Then, sure enough, everything that went up started to come down again.

Some of the rocks were heading straight at Charlie and Bear.

Charlie felt Bear grab his arm. "Charlie, we're going to run now," he said. "Just concentrate on sticking right beside me."

Together they pelted across the cold lava. Magma Quest never felt as real as this.

Crash.

Charlie heard the noise of a flying rock hitting the ground behind him. Another *crash* followed, ever closer this time. Bear was still running, not looking back, so Charlie stuck to his side and kept pushing forward. The air was full of noise and heat, then *crash-crash-crash*— it was like the volcano was machine-gunning them.

Bear guided them to a large boulder

lying on the ground.
It was about half the
size of a car and had a
large overhang. They both
skidded to a halt in its shadow
and hunched down.

Rocks rained down on the ground
all around them while they sheltered
behind the boulder. Charlie was gasping
for breath. He could see rocks landing
to the side, and he watched as each one
left a smoky trail behind it in the air, and
shattered into small pieces when it hit.
Charlie knew he was protected by the big
boulder, but he still flinched whenever
the bigger rocks hit the ground.

Eventually the rain of rocks slowed
and stopped. Bear peered out from
behind the boulder, then stood up.

"We're clear."

He smiled as Charlie got up.

"You know, volcanoes are like people," he said. "Sometimes the pressure builds up inside them and they have to let it out. They feel better once they do."

Bear might have been smiling, but Charlie was still worried. "Will it do it again?" he asked, sneaking a sideways glance at the smoking summit.

"It's impossible to tell. But there's one thing we can do."

"Keep going?"

"That's right!" Bear gave him an encouraging smile. "You've got the survival spirit, Charlie. We adapt to whatever challenge we're facing."

Bear prodded one of the fallen rock fragments with his boot. It was about the size of a man's two clenched fists.

"Before we go, take a look at this. It's pumice, like the pebbles in your pocket," he said. Charlie winced when Bear picked it up, but all the heat had gone out of it. Bear passed it gently to Charlie.

Charlie turned the rock over in his hands. It was fascinating. It felt a little bit warm, like the outside of a bowl of oatmeal, but that was all. Just now this thing in his hands had been inside a real, actual volcano. How cool was that?

"It's really light," he said. It *looked* like a rock, but it should have felt heavier than it was.

"That's because it's full of bubbles," said Bear. "When it was inside the volcano a few minutes ago it was molten magma, and it was under massive pressure. But once it was out the pressure dropped and the bubbles appeared in it, just like when you open a soda and it all sprays out. And when the lava hits the air and it cools down and turns solid, all those bubbles are trapped. That's why it cools down so quickly too – because it's full of holes. In fact, pumice can even float in water."

"Float!" Charlie exclaimed. He squinted at the rock more closely. Its surface was covered with small holes, like popped bubbles. "A rock that can float?"

"Scout's honor!" Bear promised with a smile.

Charlie looked at the

pebbles in his pocket. Sure enough, they all had tiny bubbles in them too.

"I'm going to check this," he said as he put the rock back in his pocket with the pebbles. Bear laughed.

"Be my guest. Come on – let's get going before our big friend over there decides to blow again."

They walked on, and soon enough the plain deepened into a valley. Once they were down from the lava rocks there was color everywhere. There were yellows and browns and reds, like someone had scattered mustard and curry powder over the ground. It was beautiful. Or, it would have been if it hadn't been for the smell. There was a thick steam that drifted up toward them and it stank of rotten eggs.

Beneath Charlie's boots, the rock had changed to gloopy mud. It was soft enough to leave footprints.

Bear started to walk more carefully ahead of Charlie, once more testing the ground with his stick.

"Are we back on lava?" Charlie asked anxiously.

"No, this time it's water, but we still need to be careful." Bear pointed ahead. "There's a natural spring around here, and the volcano's heating it up to boiling point. That's where the steam comes from. And the sulfur – this stuff ..." He scraped a boot through the yellow powder. "It gets carried here by the steam and left when the water dries up."

Charlie looked disappointed. He'd

been looking forward to washing some of the dust and ash from his face. Bear was smiling. "It's good news, though. Where there's water there's life. We need to check this out – but carefully!"

Charlie followed after Bear as they walked down the valley. Once again, he made very sure he only trod where Bear had gone before.

Bear stopped and pointed ahead. "Like I said, life!" In between the yellow sulfur there were green and scraggly patches of grass. "Water means plants, and plants could mean animals."

"And animals mean people?" Charlie thought out loud.

"They often do. But in a place like this, a lot of creatures will run wild. Let's see if we can …"

Bear was interrupted as a large bubble *glooped* up through the mud up ahead. It let off a puff of steam and more of the disgusting rotten-egg stink.

"Definitely steering clear of that, then," Bear said. They changed course to walk up the valley slopes, keeping well away from the boiling mud.

Charlie was the first to see the sheep. At least, he was the first one to spot the weird-looking shape on the ground. Was it grayish yellow, or yellowish gray? Whatever it was it looked like it badly needed a wash.

As they got closer they saw that it was lying on its side by a small bush. Charlie thought it might be asleep, but as they stepped up to it Charlie saw the blood. A rock – another piece of pumice – was lodged in its skull, just behind its head.

"Looks like the volcano got it when it was chucking rocks around just now," said Bear. He crouched down by the sheep's body and pulled a knife from his belt.

"Bad news for the sheep, but good news for us."

"How?" Charlie asked.

"Because the volcano's just given us our lunch," Bear replied.

8

MUTTON CHOPS

"You mean we're going to eat it?" Charlie exclaimed in horror.

Bear smiled up at him. "That's right! A couple of mutton steaks will do us nicely. And we know it's fresh and just been killed because the blood is red, not dried up. But, if you can see anything else we could eat …"

Charlie turned in a slow circle, looking up and down the valley and over the lava plain. He already knew the answer. There was nothing bigger than a clump of grass, and he wasn't going to try eating that.

"Nothing," he admitted.

Charlie watched in fascination as Bear sliced into the sheep's woolly fleece. Usually the only uncooked meat he ever saw was wrapped up in plastic in a supermarket. To his surprise, it didn't seem as gory as he thought it might.

Bear talked as he cut.

"A survivor has to take what they're given – we can't pick and choose, we need to make the most of what's available. This sheep doesn't have any further use for its body, but we do. We can be grateful that this land that we're walking across has provided us with some of its bounty, to sustain us. We'd be fools to refuse because this is a harsh place. So ..."

He cut off a chunk of mutton, and gave it to Charlie to hold while he started to cut off another. Charlie held the chunk between his fingers and studied it carefully. It was clammy and warm, and dripping with juices. It was interesting. But then a gross thought entered his head. Was he going to have to eat this lump of meat raw?

Bear cut four chunks in total, and wrapped them in a spare T-shirt from his backpack. Then they continued walking up the valley, carefully avoiding the hot mud.

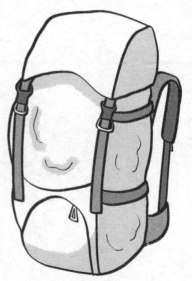

The steam got stronger, and eventually they reached a pool where the water was boiling like an angry jacuzzi. The steam billowed up in thick clouds.

"Take your boots off, Charlie," Bear said suddenly.

"Uh? We're not going to swim in that, are we?" Charlie asked, feeling worried.

"You're right, we're not going swimming here." Bear paused,

then grinned. "But once, when I was somewhere a bit like this …"

He set the T-shirt with the meat down on the ground, and sat down himself. He started to unlace his boots.

"I'd just gotten through a blizzard," Bear went on. "I was really tired and cold, and I found a volcanic hot pool like this one. What I wanted more than anything else was a good, hot bath, but I knew the water was way

too hot and I didn't fancy getting boiled. But there was also a stream of freezing-cold water nearby – melted ice from a glacier in the mountains. So what do you think I did?"

Charlie thought as he undid his boots. "You mixed them up?"

"Exactly! I dug a trench and diverted some of the freezing water into the hot pool. It cooled it down just enough for me to have the best hot bath of my life." He grinned. "Right, pass me your shoelaces."

Bear got his walking stick, and tied the ends of his and Charlie's laces around it. Then he took the four chunks of mutton, one at a time, and poked holes through them with his knife. He pushed the free ends of the laces through the holes and tied them so that the meat dangled from the end of the stick.

Charlie worked out what Bear had in mind.

"You're going to cook the sheep in the pool!" he said.

Bear smiled.

"Actually, you are!" He passed the stick to Charlie. "Lower the meat into the water, and give it about ten minutes."

Charlie took the stick and cautiously did what Bear said. The meat disappeared under the bubbling surface. This was the weirdest fishing trip ever.

"I'd prefer a nice roast," Bear said, "but we'd need a fire for that, and as you can see, we've got absolutely nothing to burn. But the earth produces more heat than we could ever need, if you know how to use it. Some countries are lucky enough to have so much volcanic activity going on that they don't need gas and electricity like other countries do. Free energy, twenty-four hours a day, seven days a week, and totally nonpolluting."

Lucky? Charlie thought. He wasn't sure he would think he was lucky to live near a volcano.

But on the other hand …

Charlie thought of Magma Quest again, as he stood, holding the stick. He was doing something else his character would never do. In the game, volcanoes were just for running around and jumping over. Until now he had never considered that a volcano could be *useful*.

Sure, the volcano could kill you if you were careless – like in the game – but if you handled it right then it could look after you too. That was just amazing.

Bear got his water bottle out of his backpack. He shook it to test how much water was in there, and made a face.

"Getting low …" He squinted at the boiling pool. "But here's not the place to fill up. Too muddy and sulfury. It's okay to cook with, but we don't want to drink a whole lot of it. Right, the meat should be done."

Charlie lifted the stick up and they both studied the pieces of mutton dangling at the end. The boiling had turned them gray. Muddy water and juices mixed together and dribbled off them. They looked disgusting, but they smelled like they were cooked.

"Sorry there's no mint sauce or potatoes," Bear said with a smile. He handed a chunk to Charlie. It squished in his fingers and the juices dripped all over his hands. Charlie was just about to take a bite when the air shook with a sound like a roar and a rumble.

The volcano was making itself known again.

A dark cloud had blown out of the top of the mountain. But for the moment, that seemed to be all it was doing. There were no more rumbles after that first one.

"Let's eat on the move, before more rocks start flying," Bear suggested.

Charlie and Bear re-laced their boots and set off quickly. They were both still clutching a piece of boiled mutton, the other two pieces wrapped in the T-shirt and stored in Bear's backpack for later.

Charlie had to concentrate to walk and eat his lunch at the same time. The mutton may have been cooked, but he had to bite hard to get a piece off. It had a weird, meaty flavor, mixed with a faint taste of sulfur. It wasn't exactly the kind of taste Charlie thought he'd ever want to experience again, but he could also feel the hot food giving him much-needed energy.

"I've never done this before," Charlie said through a mouthful.

"And maybe you never will again," Bear laughed. "That makes this occasion totally unique. There'll never be another moment like it for either of us, so let's make the most of it!"

That made Charlie think. How many times had playing games ever given him an experience he could never repeat?

Never! If he wanted to do something again in a game, all he had to do was repeat that level. Then it wasn't new anymore. But here, he was getting a new experience with every single thing he did.

Eating freshly killed, freshly boiled mutton while they tried to escape from a volcano … Bear was right. Charlie would almost certainly never do this again.

Ever since Charlie had met Bear, he had been learning that the real world had a lot more twists and surprises in it than you would find in any game.

But it also offered more opportunities for coping with them.

Just then, a sudden gust of wind blew dirt and grit into Charlie's face. His glasses protected his eyes, but his face was exposed.
It really hurt.

"Ow!"

Bear turned to him.

"There's not a lot of shelter, is there?" he said. "And the lava down here's older and crumblier. Unfortunately that means more stuff flying around when the wind gets up." He looked at Charlie. "If you can go on a bit longer, we can look for better shelter. It will be night soon. How do you feel, sport?"

"I say we go on," Charlie said.

Bear grinned.

"On to the next level!" he agreed.

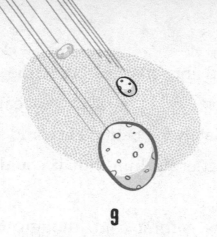

9

LAVA TUBE

As they walked on down the valley slopes, Charlie looked back up the way they had come. The black cloud was still there in the sky. It hung over them like a million tons that could fall down at any moment.

The wind that had thrown grit into Charlie's face was picking up too. A strange moan filled the air all around them. It seemed to burrow down his ears and into his head. Charlie pulled his hood up to protect his ears and immediately felt better. He could feel the wind battering him, but it couldn't get in.

It was getting cold, though. Charlie could feel the chill digging through into his bones. He started to shiver.

"We won't get far while this lasts," Bear shouted over the noise of the wind. "Let's get out of it and save our strength."

Bear and Charlie found a hollow between some boulders, where they could sit down. The hollow wasn't very deep, but even a couple of feet was deep enough for the wind to go whistling over them, not through them.

When the wind had begun to die down, Bear poked his head up.

"I think we're –"

He never finished.

BOOM!

There was no mistaking that sound. The volcano had just blown. Big time.

BOOM! ***BOOM!***

The sky started to fill with billowing clouds. Streaks of fire shot out like fireworks. The mountain was firing off missiles in all directions. Some of them were heading straight for Bear and Charlie.

Charlie was exhausted. He and Bear had walked all day, for hours on end. They had crawled through a glacier and put miles between themselves and the volcano. But the flying rocks covered that distance like it wasn't there.

And now they were right out in the

open. The hollow they were in was too shallow to give them any real shelter from above.

"We need to move," said Bear urgently. "You ready, Charlie?"

Charlie looked up at the rocks whistling through the air toward them. He wanted it all just to go away. But he knew that Bear was right. They had to use all their skill and strength to get to safety. And they only had seconds to do it.

As they ran, Charlie saw what Bear had seen. The entrance to a cave. It was round, like the entrance to a pipe. They staggered to a halt inside it, just as a pile of rocks crashed down outside.

The bombardment went on for much longer than before, and the rocks were much heavier. Charlie flinched as one of them smashed down right in front of the entrance. He pulled back a few feet to escape the ash and the flying fragments.

"I'm glad this cave was here," Charlie gasped.

Bear nodded and smiled. How did he manage to stay so calm throughout all of this?

"It's a lava tube." Bear was bending down, a few feet from the entrance. The roof was too low for him to stand up. "This whole thing used to be a stream of flowing lava, like we saw back on the mountain. When the outside edges of the lava, the bits nearest to the air, cooled down, they turned solid. That meant the inside bits could stay hot, so they kept flowing. They left this tube behind."

Charlie was looking around. "Cool," he said, though he couldn't help feeling nervous every time another rock crashed down outside the cave.

He backed farther into the cave, and when there was a break between explosions outside, he heard something new. It was the sound of running water.

Charlie remembered something. His dad liked to drink mineral water, and the label on the bottle always said "filtered through volcanic rock."

He found where the noise was coming from. The water wasn't flowing fast, but it would fill a bottle soon enough.

"Hey," Charlie said, "the water in this cave should be clean, right? I mean, nothing to make us ill?"

"One hundred percent pure," Bear agreed with a smile. He tipped out the old water from his bottle and passed it to Charlie.

Charlie felt pretty

pleased as he held the bottle under the trickling water. He was problem solving to help them survive, just like Bear.

They both took a deep drink, then Charlie refilled the bottle. They sat, watching the rocks fall down outside.

If one of those things hits us, Charlie thought, *we'll be dead for sure.*

But that wasn't going to happen because along with chucking out all that dangerous rock and ash, the volcano had also provided this place to shelter, as well as clean, filtered water to drink.

Nature just gave you stuff, Charlie realized. It was up to you what you did with it. If you handled it right, then you lived. You didn't need any fake antigravity or super strength. You just needed yourself. You didn't need to earn it, or pay for it, you just had to keep your eyes open and use what it offered.

In his time with Bear, Charlie had

used his brain and body together. He had solved problems and gotten through sticky situations. It hadn't been a made-up game character doing that. It had been *him*, Charlie.

That was just amazing.

Crash –

> *crash –*

>> *crash –*

CRASH!

Suddenly the tube filled up with a flying cloud of ash. It stung Charlie's eyes and his chest heaved as he started to cough and sneeze. His eyes streamed and blinded him.

He felt a hand hit his back between his shoulder blades.

"Charlie? Are you all right?"

"Yeah," Charlie gasped. "It was just the smoke …"

"I know," said the voice. "You should take more care around bonfires."

10

ANTIGRAVITY

"Bonfires?"

Charlie kept blinking until his eyes had been washed clean and he could open them again. He could breathe freely, although his mouth tasted of ash.

But it wasn't Bear pounding his back. It was a leader from camp. And he wasn't in the lava tube anymore. He was back in the clearing at camp, next to the smoking campfire.

There was no sign of Bear, no sign of any flying rocks, or ash, or lava, or the volcano.

"If you're playing capture the flag you'd better get going," the leader said. "I can see someone coming. Good luck – and stay away from bonfires!"

Harry and Mia had appeared at the edge of the trees. Neither of them were wearing armbands. They had both been caught and converted into guardians.

"*Get him!*" Harry shouted, a huge grin spread wide across his face.

Charlie was already running. Sure, the volcano thing

was confusing, but he was still in the game and he wanted to stay that way. One thing Charlie did know was how to play to win.

Trees flew past. Charlie could hear Harry and Mia, running and laughing behind him. Charlie was grinning too. This was so cool.

He could smell the dry leaves that his running feet kicked up. The patterns made by beams of sunlight shining through the leaves flashed past his eyes.

Everything felt super real. Everything felt alive.

It was all so different from the massive volcano and the lava plains – but somehow it was the same too. It was all part of nature. It was all there for him to enjoy. Everywhere you looked, there was something different and new. He felt full of life. There were no special game powers here. Just his own body doing what it could, pushed to the max. Until . . .

"Gotcha!" Harry shouted happily, catching him and ripping his armband off.

"Aw ..." Charlie grumbled, but he could still feel the big smile on his face.

Mia caught up to them. She was holding something.

"Charlie, this fell out of your pocket," she said, and passed Charlie his tablet. "It looks okay, though."

Charlie's eyes opened wide.

"Oh, man! I'd be in such trouble if I lost that. Thanks."

He tucked it gratefully into his pocket. That was weird. He hadn't even noticed it was with him, let alone that it had fallen out.

They took a moment to get their breath.

"So, there's three of us," Mia said.

"And only two of them!" Harry shouted, spotting some other runners with armbands nearby. "Get them!"

Laughing, they chased through the woods.

Charlie and Harry and Mia were still laughing as they piled a mountain of sandwiches on their plates at lunchtime and sat down at a table with Joe and Olly.

"So, Joe, what's your secret?" Harry said. "What's your special ninja capture the flag trick for not getting caught?"

Joe had been crowned champion of the game, but he looked a bit embarrassed.

"I, uh, kind of call it … getting lost."

They all stared at him and he shrugged.

"I guess I don't have a sense of direction, you know? I thought I was heading for the base … turned out I was going completely the wrong way! So, no one saw me."

"Sounds like you need a better compass," Harry said cheerfully.

Olly had finished and stood up to go. "Want to play Magma Quest later, Charlie?" he asked. "Show me how to finish the lava level?"

Charlie smiled.

"Sure, anytime..." He felt the tablet knock against something else in his pocket. What was that? He pulled it out and stared at it as the other boys started to leave.

A small, gray pebble, covered with little holes.

It was pumice – exactly like one of the pebbles Charlie had used to navigate with Bear.

Could it really be? The way it felt in his hand was so familiar ...

Okay, Charlie decided, *let's test it.*

"I'll, uh, catch up, guys," he said.

Bear had said pumice floated in water. There was a half-empty water pitcher on the drinks table. Feeling a bit silly, he held the pebble over the water. Then he let go.

Plop.

The pebble sank down to the bottom of the pitcher – and then bobbed up again. It floated just under the surface of the water.

It was pumice! It really did float. It had its own antigravity in water!

Wow. He really *had* been on the volcano.

"Oh, that's disgusting, Charlie!" someone snapped. "I was just about to pour a drink!"

Charlie looked up in surprise. Evie was standing by him.

"Oh, sorry," he said. "I thought everyone had gone."

He started to fish the stone out of the pitcher. Evie yelped.

"Don't put your fingers in it!"

It was too late. A bit embarrassed, Charlie took the pumice out and wiped it on his pants. Evie looked disgusted with him.

"I could get you a drink from the sink?" he offered, to make up for it.

"Okay," she said. "Thanks."

Charlie brought a fresh glass of water back to where Evie sat on her own with her small plate of food.

"Here you are," he said.

"I made sure it was a clean glass," he added, to reassure her. Some instinct made Charlie sit down with Evie. She was on her own and she looked lonely. He remembered she had been like this at breakfast too. Evie took so long to choose her food that everyone else was finished before she had even started.

"So, what are you doing after lunch?" he asked.

"Haven't decided," she told him. "I might do the construction challenge."

There wasn't much on her plate and

Evie pecked at it slowly, like she really didn't like it. Charlie remembered how much he had enjoyed wolfing down a mountain of food. He smiled to himself as he remembered the dead sheep boiled in the volcanic hot pool. She'd never believe him if he told her, and she'd certainly never eat anything that looked so disgusting!

Then the idea struck Charlie. It was so simple and so brilliant.

Charlie could introduce Evie to Bear. But how?

He thought back to the clearing. Somehow, Charlie had gone from there to the volcano. The bonfire had blown smoke, and when it cleared, there he was.

Would it work if he took Evie to the

clearing? But then, how would he make the smoke happen again? What were the rules to get to Bear? He knew there was something he was missing.

Then he remembered the compass. It had gone all weird and spun around between the five directions. Hmm. But it had worked fine on the lava plain. Did the fifth direction lead to Bear?

Charlie got the compass out and looked at it. The needle was still, but perhaps it was worth a try.

He passed it to Evie.

"You know – whatever you do this afternoon, this might be useful," he said.

Evie picked it up curiously.

"Thanks. Do you want to swap something for it?"

Charlie smiled and shook his head.

"It's okay," he said. "Just consider it a gift."

The End

Bear Grylls got the taste for adventure at a young age from his father, a former Royal Marine. After school, Bear joined the Reserve SAS, then went on to become one of the youngest people ever to climb Mount Everest, just two years after breaking his back in three places during a parachute jump.

Among other adventures he has led expeditions to the Arctic and the Antarctic, crossed oceans and set world records in skydiving and paragliding.

Bear is also a bestselling author and the host of television programs such as *Survival School* and *The Island*.

He has shared his survival skills with people all over the world, and has taken many famous movie stars and sports stars on adventures – and even President Barack Obama!

Bear Grylls is Chief Scout to the UK Scouting Association, encouraging young people to have great adventures, follow their dreams and to look after their friends. Bear is also honorary Colonel to the Royal Marine Commandos.

When Bear's not traveling the world, he lives with his wife and three sons on a barge in London, or on an island off the coast of Wales.

Find out more at **www.beargrylls.com**

DID YOU KNOW?

- There are about 1,500 active volcanos on Earth, and over 400 of them are in the Pacific Ocean, in an arc shape known as the "Ring of Fire."

- Inside a volcano, the boiling liquid rock is called magma. Once it explodes out of the volcano, it is called lava.

- The word "volcano" comes from Vulcan, who was the Roman god of fire.

- There are volcanos all around the solar system too – the moons of Jupiter, Saturn and Neptune all have active volcanos.